CHAPTER 1

"Take a look at this, Josh. It's REALLY cool. Come on, just pause the game for a minute."

Scott was waving something silver in front of his little brother's face. It was an odd looking stick covered with small blue stars that glowed.

"I can't look now, so quit bugging me! I'm trying to capture the dragon in *The Fight for Magicallus* and this is my highest score ever." Josh never took his eyes off the computer screen. His fingers jumped around on the controls.

"But Josh," Scott insisted, "You're gonna like this. I traded my Derek Jeter autographed baseball card to Nick and he gave me this magic wand from Germany. Anyway it's my turn to play; you've been hogging the game for an hour."

Josh didn't bother to answer, he was concentrating too hard. His eyes followed the green and blue dragon on the screen. It was breathing fire and growing bigger and stronger. A knight was fighting the dragon with a battleax and a lance. With every blow, the knight grew bigger and the dragon grew smaller. Scott was growing irritated. He waved the wand over his brother's head.

smaller. Scott was growing irritated. He waved the wand over his brother's head.

"Hocus Pocus, try to focus. Josh, look here or you'll disappear."

The room suddenly went dark and strangely quiet. After a minute the lights flickered and came back on. Scott dropped the wand yelling, "Ow! My hand is burning!" The wand lay glowing on the floor, its stars fluttering like butterflies. Scott looked around; he was alone in the room. His hand really hurt and he was in no mood for jokes. Scott did not deal well with pain.

"Josh, where are you? Quit goofing around!"

No answer. Scott's brown eyes widened with surprise. He pushed his wavy black hair back from his face and walked from his bedroom to the hallway and into the family room. Josh was nowhere to be found. His mom was in the kitchen cooking dinner and it smelled delicious. Spaghetti with garlic rolls was his favorite.

He poked his head in, "Mom, have you seen Josh?"

His mother looked up from the sauce she was stirring and smiled.

"Isn't he with you?" she asked, handing him a warm garlic roll. Scott ate it in two bites and licked his fingers. As she talked, she sliced carrots for the salad.

"Listen Scott, Dad will be home soon so finish up your game. I swear you're both going to go blind sitting in front of that computer all the time. You boys should ride bikes or read a book once in a while." She shook her head and sighed deeply for effect.

"Yes Mom." Scott had heard this lecture before. He raced back to the bedroom, still no Josh. He looked under the bed and in the closet. He was looking behind the door when he happened to glance at the computer screen and his mouth fell open. There was the dragon, still breathing fire and looking ferocious but the knight fighting him wasn't Sir Edward the Fearless. It was Josh! He was still dressed in his favorite camp shirt, red shorts and sneakers but he was only 2" tall! Sure Josh had always been smaller than other seven-year-old kids but this was just crazy.

"But...how? What is going on?" Scott sputtered. He started shaking the computer monitor and shouting as loudly as he could, "JOSH, JOSH CAN YOU HEAR ME?"

His mother yelled back from the kitchen. "The whole neighborhood can hear you, honey."

This can't be happening, Scott thought, starting to sweat. He had to try to undo whatever it was he'd done. Scott gingerly picked up the wand and pointing it at his teeny tiny brother said: "Hocus Pocus try to focus. Josh reappear and come back here!"

The wand began to vibrate and hum and a soft cloud of greenish mist formed in front of the computer screen-but nothing else happened. When the mist cleared, Scott was horrified to see the dragon closing in on Josh who was out of weapons! Scott tossed the wand aside, grabbed the controller and started to play the game. Most times, he could beat the dragon at this level. He really hoped this was one of those times. The dragon's fiery breath was almost touching Josh's chest. Scott couldn't let that happen or the game would be over and his little brother would be toast! He was so nervous he bit his lip until he drew blood. Playing with a concentration far beyond his ten years, Scott worked the controls until finally, exhausted, he was able to re-arm Josh with a battleax. At least his brother was no longer defenseless, he thought.

It was all up to Josh now. Scott watched the screen intently; afraid to blink for fear he would miss something. While Josh slashed furiously at the dangerous dragon looming over him,

Scott chewed on his nails. With each blow of Josh's battleax, the terrible beast shrank back, its firepower weakening. Meanwhile, Josh was growing steadily, and by the time he defeated the dragon, he was a full three inches tall. Only four feet to go and he will be back to himself, Scott thought. The once fearsome dragon was now small enough to be Josh's pet Chihuahua. Scott was relieved to see that its breath wouldn't even light a match. He watched as Josh turned towards the creature, swung his right foot all the way back and kicked the dragon so hard it broke into a million particles of light. Josh then grinned at Scott and gave him thumbs up. This made Scott laugh out loud.

In the kitchen, their mother was happy to hear them having such a good time. At least when they played computer games they were more animated than when they watched T.V. She had no idea just how animated her youngest son was at that moment.

Back in the bedroom, Scott's happiness was short-lived. Hideous goblins were creeping up on Josh from all sides but of course he wasn't paying attention. He was too busy trying to communicate with Scott using weird sign language. First, he pointed at the ground and then pointed at himself. Next, he shook his head "no" while jumping high in the air and pulling his hair straight up. Scott, who had absolutely no idea what his brother was trying to say, began yelling at the screen, "Look out Josh, behind you!" Although Josh could see Scott, it seemed he couldn't hear him. Scott was frantic. He'd never seen goblins in this game and had no idea what to do. He tried all the buttons on the controller in every combination but nothing worked. The goblins were even closer now.

Convinced that there was no time to waste, Scott made a decision. He grabbed the wand off the floor, pointed it at himself and in a shaky voice, said: "Hocus Pocus try to focus, Scott look here or you'll disappear."

Instantly, he found himself in total darkness, spinning around uncontrollably like water being sucked down the drain of a bathtub. The force of it was making him sick to his stomach. Scott held onto the wand as tightly as he could and right before he passed out, whispered, "I hope this isn't going to hurt."

CHAPTER 2

When he opened his eyes, Scott was amazed by the bizarre colors around him. Trees were purple with vivid orange leaves; the grass was neon blue and the sky was yellow and cloudless. There was no sun yet everything was painfully bright. Scott took a deep breath and let it out. He could smell absolutely nothing: no flowers, no trees and certainly no spaghetti with garlic rolls. Sitting up slowly, Scott tried to take inventory of every bruise and bump. Surprisingly he felt alright, just a bit lightheaded. Actually, he felt light all over. Standing up, he took a step and effortlessly leaped several feet into the air like an astronaut walking on the moon. It was *so* cool. His body shimmered as if he were made of nothing more than light. Scott *really* didn't want to dwell on that. To his relief, he still had the wand which now resembled a piece of red licorice. As Scott watched, the stars changed into crawling black spiders that tickled his hand. But where was Josh? Did the goblins get him? Was Scott too late to save his little brother?

Someone tapped him forcefully on the shoulder but when Scott turned around, nobody was there.

"Is that you Josh?"

He didn't recognize his own voice. He sounded like Alvin or one of the Chipmunks. Again someone tapped him on the shoulder. Spinning around, he found himself nose to nose with a goblin. Scott's nerves could take no more and an incredibly loud scream erupted from him. It seemed to start from the soles of his feet and gain strength on the way up. His new Chipmunk voice must have been quite shrill because the little blue goblin bellowed in pain and ran away with his hands covering his hairy ears. Scott stopped screaming and stared at the retreating monster in disbelief. It was hiding behind the closest purple tree. He slowly approached the nervous creature and spoke in a soothing voice.

"Hello? Are you okay in there? I'm sorry if I scared you but you did scare me first. I'm not sure if you can understand what I'm saying but I'm trying to find my little brother. His name is Josh and he looks like me only a lot shorter. Have you seen him?"

The goblin cautiously stepped out from behind the tree. Standing only as high as Scott's shoulder, he looked even smaller close up. The goblin's clothing consisted of a long blue vest that reached to his equally blue thighs. Aside from his hairy ears and bushy eyebrows, he had no 1 other hair. His large green eyes were set far apart and his face looked flattened as if it were pressed against a window. Although this goblin may have been handsome in his mother's eyes, he was quite ugly by human standards, yet Scott thought he looked kind. When he spoke, his mouth twisted into a smile.

"I dare say that was not the most civilized way to introduce yourself, young man, that screaming in my ear business." He had a pleasant voice with an English accent.

"You did give me quite a fright but I accept your apology as you seem sincere." The creature studied him openly.

8

"Hmmm...this is very curious indeed. You are clearly not a goblin yet you could not be mistaken for a knight either...well, no matter."

He grabbed Scott's hand and began shaking it vigorously. The handshake gave Scott a mild electric shock and he yanked his hand away.

"Hey, that hurt!"

"So sorry, it seems that you carry a positive charge. You really should have warned me. Now, I would be happy to help you look for your brother but I implore you, please stop screaming. Goblins have extremely sensitive ears." He tugged on his ears for emphasis and smiled broadly at Scott. "But where are my manners? I never even introduced myself! How unforgivable. My name is Vxngrtl and I am *delighted* to make your acquaintance."

"Your name is Vexing Girdle? Can I just call you Vex?"

"That would be fine, and you are...?"

"Scott."

The goblin burst out laughing but pretended it was just a bad coughing fit.

"*What* is so funny?" Scott asked.

"I don't mean to be impolite dear boy, but your name is rather humorous. In these parts "Skot" means 'he who finds vegetables too disgusting for words'." He started to laugh all over again then had to wipe the tears from his eyes. "I do apologize."

Scott was sure he heard Vex chuckling quietly to himself as they started out together on the shining yellow path that was the only visible road. They walked for some time and although they covered several feet with each giant step, they never seemed to advance and the landscape never changed. Off in the distance, the occasional knight would ride by on horseback, his shield gleaming with reflected light.

"Vex, why don't we ask those knights if they've seen Josh?"

The goblin looked horrified at the prospect.

"That would be more than foolish Scott; it would be the end of us."

Vex would say no more about it and they kept moving forward. After what seemed a long while, Scott leaped high in the air and craned his neck to look around. The path had neither beginning nor end; it just seemed to stretch on forever. Scott was becoming impatient; he needed to find Josh sooner rather than later.

"Vex?"

"Yes?"

"Where are we going?"

"I believe we are on our way to find your brother."

"But we don't seem to be getting anywhere."

"Of course we are, haven't we been walking continuously? I'm certain he'll pop up at any moment, don't worry."

"But Vex, the last time I saw him, he was surrounded by goblins."

Vex stopped short and threw up his hands.

"Why did you neglect to tell me this? It changes everything!"

Looking annoyed Vex abruptly left the path. He walked exactly ten paces and, with his arms at his sides, he began to spin like a top faster and faster until he was just a blur. A hole was opening up under the goblin's feet and he was sinking into the ground. Neon blue grass was flying everywhere. Scott began to panic. He hadn't meant to upset Vex and he definitely didn't want to be left behind. Just as Vex disappeared from view, Scott held his breath and jumped into the hole feet first, clutching the wand with both hands. He was in free fall, screaming all the way down until he hit the bottom with a thud.

CHAPTER 3

SCOTT LAY ON THE GROUND DAZED, WONDERING WHY HE wasn't as light as air anymore.

"You forgot already!" Vex teased as he walked towards his companion.

"What did I forget?" Scott whispered still trying to catch his breath.

"Why, my sensitive ears of course. You screamed all the way here but I will forgive you once again." Vex smiled fondly.

The more time Scott spent with Vex, the less ugly the goblin seemed. His face is growing on me, Scott thought and then he smiled at his choice of words wondering how his parents would react if Vex's face *really* "grew" on him? "This is our son Scott, he didn't always look like a pug dog with a squished in face but something strange happened and, well, we love him anyway..."

"Welcome to the Cavern of the Goblins, Scott. Although we don't receive many visitors, we're happy when they find their way here."

Scott looked around in amazement. The walls and ceiling

were sparkling with a dazzling blue light that illuminated the entire cavern. It was enormous. Along the walls, there were dozens of triangular shaped tables and chairs all made of the same brilliant material. Scott wished he had his sunglasses.

"I guess your eyes aren't as sensitive as your ears, Vex."

Vex laughed. "Clever observation, my boy. Everything here is made out of blue diamonds; they are quite common at this depth and grow by the thousands. We build with them, use them for lighting and we even eat them-which accounts for the goblins' lovely blue color." He demonstrated by plucking a diamond off the wall and nibbling on it delicately.

"Would you care to try one? They are delicious."

Scott shuddered. "No thanks. Unless you can offer me one of the four major food groups: pizza, French fries, cookies or ice cream, I'll pass. Sorry to change the subject but do you really think Josh is down here?"

"I think there's a good chance of it," Vex assured him. "This cavern is home to a hundred goblins; surely one of them has seen him. Let's start in the game room where goblins meet to play challenging games of strategy. You will find that goblins are highly intelligent and quite sophisticated." Scott shook his head muttering, "You forgot modest."

Vex led the way through several long corridors that twisted and turned in unexpected ways. As they walked, Scott saw dozens of orange bat-like creatures hanging from the ceiling in a sleepy sort of way. They made no noise and barely moved at all. In fact, Scott could hear nothing but the sound of his own footsteps echoing off the walls.

"Vex...where are the other ninety-nine goblins that live here? Is it naptime or something?"

"I was just wondering that myself," he replied looking puzzled. "It does seem odd that we haven't encountered anyone."

He shrugged his shoulders and kept walking at a rapid pace, frequently zigging or zagging without warning. Scott was practically running to keep up when the goblin suddenly stopped and Scott crashed right into him. Unfazed, Vex announced "Ah, here we are at the game room."

Pausing at the door, he whispered somewhat dramatically, "When we go in, please keep your voice down. My colleagues insist on absolute quiet when they are concentrating on their games."

With this, he gently opened the shiny blue door, and then stood there motionless, gaping at the sight before him. The room, which was about the size of a school cafeteria, was jam-packed with goblins of all shapes and sizes, in every shade of blue. They were cheering and yelling wildly and there even seemed to be some betting going on. All eyes were turned toward the center of the room.

Scott yelled to Vex over the noisy crowd, "Let's get closer and see what your 'sophisticated' friends are doing." Vex nodded, a shocked look on his face.

They began weaving their way through the mob. Although the noise level was incredible Vex didn't seem to notice and his companion wondered if delicate goblin ears were in fact a myth. Scott could feel the excitement coursing through the room and it occurred to him that this crowd was no different than the crowds at football and soccer games. He finally understood what his Dad meant when he said: "give the people bread and circuses and they're happy." Scott supposed this saying could just as easily apply to goblins-although he wasn't sure if they ate bread. His thoughts were suddenly interrupted by Vex shouting, "Scott watch out!"

It was too late. As Scott turned, a flying object hit him square on the back of the head. *Why does this always happen to me?* He thought, rubbing his sore head. For a guy with a low tolerance for pain, he sure was getting his share. Vex eventually arrived at Scott's side, having squeezed through the crowd. He would have gotten there sooner but he was too polite to push or shove. The goblin examined the missile. It was a piece of a chair.

"Scott, I am *deeply* sorry for your injury. You must think we are all hooligans and ruffians, and rightly so! I wish I could explain this madness, but I simply cannot. Who could be so barbaric as to break chairs and throw them about? This is unacceptable!" All of this came out as one sentence and Vex had to stop to catch his breath.

Scott smiled weakly, "I'm okay Vex, don't worry. I haven't got a clue why chairs are flying, I don't live here, remember?"

"I really must see what is going on. Are you feeling well enough to proceed, my boy?"

Scott nodded and they inched their way forward again. Surprisingly, all it took was one push against an unyielding goblin to propel Scott through. Off balance, he stumbled and dropped to his knees where he found it easier to crawl between the distracted goblins. Scott didn't realize he had finally reached the center of the room. He stood up and found himself surrounded by goblins in strange costumes that paid no attention to him at all; they were too busy fighting with each other. One goblin in a badly constructed suit of armor was locked in combat with a thin dark goblin in a tall hat. The thin one grabbed the other and swung him around in what looked like a "helicopter spin".

Nearby, two smaller goblins were dressed in capes and masks like superheroes and one was giving the other a"piledriver". That was Scott's favorite move...how would these goblins know anything about professional wrestling?

The crowd was cheering and things were flying around, what a free-for-all! It reminded Scott of the food fight in the school cafeteria the week before. Nick had been throwing peas at Mark who returned fire with a volley of tater tots and, before long, everyone had jumped in. Nick was quite proud of the commotion he had caused and said it was definitely worth going to detention. Scott smiled. It seemed like a long time since he'd seen his friends.

Vex was fuming when he finally caught up to Scott. "Look at this chaos! It is a dark day indeed for the Goblins of the Cavern. I am simply appalled...just a moment, what is that I see?" He peered through the densely packed goblins. "I cannot believe it! Scott, do you see a purple cloak way over there?" He pointed toward the opposite side of the room where a cloaked figure stood in the shadows.

"That cloak is so special that it may only be worn by one who performs a great service for the goblins. I know of no such individual and yet...the fact remains, someone is wearing the Cloak of Honor." At that moment Vex recognized a short round goblin passing by and unceremoniously grabbed him by the arm.

"Here is someone who can explain everything, I am sure of it. Scott, this is 'Smrkngcw,' one of our respected elder states-men. Smrkngcw, may I present to you a fine gentleman, his name is Scott. He is not from around these parts so you mustn't shake his hand."

Scott was careful to keep his hands by his side, "Nice to meet you Mr. "Smirking Cow"".

The roundish goblin beamed at them both and, without a word, pulled the startled Vex into a bear hug and spun him around several times before releasing him.

"Vxngrtl old man!" he cried out in a booming voice. "I'm terribly happy to see you again! How are you enjoying the festivities? Jolly good time isn't it? This wrestling business is *such* fun. I am enjoying it even more than Poker, the other game I learned today. And now I do believe it's my turn to be in the ring. Of course, you and your friend will want to join in so what say we find you some costumes?"

Scott whispered "Is this guy drunk, or what?"

The look on Vex's face was one of disbelief; he was clearly speechless. Hearing no response, Scott turned to Smirking Cow and asked a pointed question.

"Could you tell me who is wearing the Cloak of Honor and what service he performed for the goblins?"

"Certainly, I would be glad to tell you although...I'm a bit hazy on the details. I'm told he comes from far away and has a funny name. Wait, it's coming to me...oh what is his name? I've got it! It's 'Lord Magic, the Undefeated'. He is not a knight of course because everyone knows knights despise goblins. No knight would even *consider* slaying the dragon that plagued us. But Lord Magic, now there's a brave fellow. I hear it was quite a show when he trounced that dastardly dragon, Chimera. I am sorry I missed it, at the time I was..." Smirking Cow's voice trailed off as he realized he was talking to no one. Vexing Girdle and his friend were gone. He shrugged and went off to practice his moves.

CHAPTER 4

Across the room, Lord Magic, as he called himself, was surrounded by admirers and well-wishers. He was handing out small objects which the goblins were eagerly snatching from his hand. As they moved closer, Scott and Vex could hear what Lord Magic was saying even though his back was towards them.

"That one is cherry flavor and this one is sour apple. Hey, no pushing! Just wait your turn. " Lord Magic's voice was high-pitched like Scott's.

"Have we found your brother at last?" Vex asked hopefully.

Scott shook his head. "It can't be him; this guy is way too tall to be Josh."

At this, Lord Magic spun around. "Smooth move, Scott, why did you follow me here?"

"Josh? Is that really you? I've been looking for you everywhere. Don't worry, I'm here to rescue you."

"Scott, do I look like I need rescuing? Things are going great! I'm tall now and I've got all these cool goblin dudes to hang around with. I'm their hero. And the coolest thing of all is that I am inside *The Fight for Magicallus*. I'm not going anywhere. Maybe *you're* the one who needs rescuing."

Scott was fuming. After all he had been through to find Josh!

"How about a little more gratitude and a little less attitude?"

"You're just jealous," Josh responded.

"Am not!"

"You are!"

"Not!"

"Are too."

Vex cleared his throat. "Excuse me but how long will this, um, exchange continue?"

Scott thought about it. "We usually keep going until our Dad makes us stop."

"I see...well, in that case, do carry on."

"Forget it now Vex, you just took all the fun out of it." Scott looked at Josh and grinned. "You sure have a squeaky voice for such a tall guy."

"Well at least I don't sound like Mickey Mouse."

They both started laughing. "How did you get so tall anyway, Josh?"

"Remember when I was fighting the dragon? I just kept growing."

"Oh, I see. And what was with that sign language stuff? What exactly was your point?"

"You couldn't understand that? First, I pointed at the ground and then at myself-that meant I'm staying right here. Then I shook my head 'no', pulled my hair and jumped up. That meant: don't-pull me-out of here. Get it? I *thought* it was easy but I guess not."

"You know I hate playing Charades, I'm much better at

crossword puzzles. So what did you do to these goblins? They are all acting crazy."

At this, Vex jumped into the conversation. "Yes, indeed. I too would like to hear this story."

"I gave them my jelly beans."

Scott was incredulous. "*You* gave away candy? The Josh I know would never do that. Are you sure you're my brother?" He was only half-joking.

"If you want me to prove it I can tell everyone about the time you ripped your pants at school in front of all the girls and-"

Scott cut him off. "Fine, you're Josh."

"Anyway, I had to give away my candy. I lost to these guys in poker."

Scott snickered while Vex looked perplexed. The goblin to Josh's right giggled and said, "That's right, he taught us how to play and we taught him how to lose!"

"That is no way to treat an honored guest," Vex chided him.

"Yeah, buzz off already," Josh snapped and the goblin walked away gleefully counting his jelly beans and the other goblins followed. Now they could talk without being disturbed.

CHAPTER 5

Scott looked *up* at his younger brother. It felt strange to look up, since he'd always had to look down before. Of course, everything in this place was strange and he was ready to get the heck out of there.

"Josh, get real, you can't stay here forever. What about school?"

As soon as he said it, Scott realized this was not his best argument. His brother just rolled his eyes and made a funny face. Vex watched their exchange with interest, his head turning from one to the other as if he were watching a tennis match.

"Okay you're right, forget about school, no more school, hooray. But what about your friends, don't you want to see them again?"

"I can make new friends."

"Maybe you can, maybe you can't. But, what about the dog? Mom and Dad only got him because you nagged them for two years. Won't you miss Sunny?"

"Oh, for sure."

"Then you want to go home?"

"That would be no."

Scott threw up his hands. "I give up. You can stay for all I care. If you want to make Mom cry, that's your choice. I'll just keep all your toys and now I'll be the one building stuff with Dad in the garage-since you won't be there to butt in."

Josh thought for a long minute. "Okay, okay, I'll go but there's one condition."

Scott was ready to agree to anything at that point but he couldn't let Josh know. He understood his brother too well. Not only did Josh see everything as an opportunity, he was also quite tricky. Scott pretended to be indignant.

"Unbelievable! I risk my life to come rescue you and now you're adding conditions?"

Josh was unimpressed. "Actually, we wouldn't be here at all if it weren't for you. I *could* tell Mom and Dad how it was all your fault we got stuck in here in the first place. *If* we ever get out."

Scott accepted defeat, but remained cautious. "Alright so what's the one condition?"

"You give me all your turns on *The Fight for Magicallus*."

Vex stood on his tiptoes to whisper in Scott's ear. "What is this *Fight for Magicallus*?"

"It's a game," Scott whispered before turning back to Josh. "For how long?"

"A year," Josh said without missing a beat.

"A month."

"Six months."

Scott crossed his arms. "Three months and that's my final offer. Deal?"

"Deal." Josh smiled triumphantly. "You're way too easy; I would have done it for two."

"Great, then if you're so smart how about getting us out of here?"

"Me? You're the one who brought us here, you dweeb! You get us out!"

Vex stepped between the brothers. "Please remain calm, I will assist you in any way I can." Vex bowed to Josh. "Master Joshua, my name is Vxngrtl and it is truly an honor to meet you. It is not every day that I find myself in the presence of a mighty dragon slayer and Champion of the Goblins."

Scott rolled his eyes while Josh looked quite pleased with himself.

"Thanks, nice to meet you too."

Vex turned and addressed them both. "In order to help you, I need to know where you came from."

"Our house," Josh said.

"In Florida," Scott added.

Vex looked perplexed.

"In the United States of America," Josh elaborated.

"On the planet Earth," Scott said jokingly.

There was no response. "In the Milky Way Galaxy..." his voice trailed off when he saw Vex still did not understand. He had an idea. "Vex, why don't you tell us where we are now?"

"We are in the Cavern of the Goblins in the land of Magicallus." Vex's face darkened. "We have no ruler at this time and our land is in a state of turmoil. I'm sorry to report that the knights and the goblins are on the verge of war."

"Vex," Scott said gently, "I don't know how to tell you this but right now all of us are inside a computer game called *The Fight for Magicallus.*"

The goblin shook his head vigorously. "Impossible! That *cannot* be true. What foolishness is this? A game indeed! You are asking me to believe that my entire world exists as a child's *plaything*?"

"It's not just a kid's game," Josh commented, "Adults like it too."

Vex looked stricken.

"You are not helping the situation." Scott glared at his brother.

The goblin was deep in thought for several minutes. When he finally spoke, he looked serious. "Although I am certain you believe this, I cannot accept it. How can you be sure that *your* world is not merely a child's game?"

Josh shrugged. Scott looked thoughtful then he answered. "I guess we can't be sure but would it change anything? Probably not. We would still go to school every day, hang out with our friends and go home. It's like those people who are always saying the end of the world is coming, you just have to go on living your life."

"I suppose you are right." The goblin relaxed a little but then grew agitated again. He paced back and forth while he talked. "Assuming just for a moment that we are inside this *Fight for Magicallus*, what would become of my world if the game were destroyed?"

The brothers exchanged a look. "We don't know what would happen if *one* copy of the game were destroyed," Josh said. "There are *thousands* of copies out there."

Vex's mouth dropped open and his eyes bulged out-which Scott thought did not improve his looks in the slightest. The poor creature looked like he was suffering from information overload.

Looking shaken, he asked "How exactly did you travel from your world to mine?"

"With this," Scott replied, reaching into his back pocket for the wand. He quickly pulled his hand away.

"Ouch! I think it bit me!"

He reached for the wand again and again but each time it either wiggled away or bit him. Josh was losing his patience.

"Scott, what *is* the problem? I'm getting old over here. We already missed dinner, now we're going to miss breakfast too."

"I can't get it! Why don't you go ahead and try 'mighty dragon slayer'?"

Josh walked behind Scott and with no effort at all, grabbed the wand from his pocket and showed it to Vex. Not only did the wand behave itself but as soon as Josh touched it, its original silver color returned in a brilliant flash of light.

Instantly, all of the goblins stopped fighting and yelling and a hush fell over the crowd.

A goblin gasped, it was Vex. He stammered "how did you...? Where did you get 'Ex Libris'? It is the most powerful magic in the land. It has been lost ever since Sir Gilcrest disappeared."

Scott threw up his hands, "I made a bad deal, that's how I ended up with this crazy wand. I probably should have stayed in bed this morning. Maybe I *am* still in bed. If I close my eyes, will you guys still be here when I open them? Silly question. Here's another silly question, why is the wand called 'Ex Libris'?"

Vex looked around nervously and when he spoke, it was barely a whisper. "I don't know why but I do know this. Ex Libris can destroy an entire city in the time it takes to utter these words and then bring it back again unharmed. I dare say you should treat this wand with the utmost respect."

CHAPTER 6

WHEN VEX FINISHED SPEAKING, THERE WAS A LONG silence and then the room began to hum with conversation. The humming became buzzing as the goblins grew more and more upset. Suddenly a piercing scream echoed through the room. It was Smirking Cow and he was running towards Scott and Josh as fast as his round little legs would carry him. The crown sitting crookedly on his head was comical but the crazy look in his eyes was not. His blue face was almost purple with the effort of screaming at the top of his lungs while running at full speed. He tackled Josh and tried to grab the wand. Instantly a bolt of green lightning leaped from the wand and struck Smirking Cow with such force that he was knocked backward twenty feet. He lay there motionless. Dozens of goblins came rushing over to tend to him. Josh was unharmed although he did have a distinct green glow about him.

"Josh, you killed him!" Scott cried out.

"It's not my fault!" Josh protested with tears in his eyes. "He freaked out and the wand took over. It had nothing to do with me."

"It had everything to do with you," Vex replied with a strange look on his face. "The wand was protecting you."

Smirking Cow groaned loudly and sat up rubbing his head. He looked around with his crazy eyes and began ranting. "The end has come! Ex Libris will destroy us all! brother goblins, we must not let the prophecy come to pass!"

A voice yelled out: "Smirking Cow is right, we are doomed! When the knights learn we have Ex Libris they will stop at nothing until they have it. They will rule the world!"

Josh raised his hand as if he were in class and wanted the teacher to pick him. He forgot he was holding the wand and when he held it high, it sizzled and crackled with green light. The goblins shrank back from him in fear. Josh became flustered and turned to his brother for help.

"Scott, would you please talk to them?"

Reluctantly, Scott stepped forward. "Hey everyone, I have great news!" he announced brightly. "The knights don't have Ex Libris. Do you know what that means?" He paused for effect. "It means the goblins rule! Hooray for the goblins!"

A sea of blue faces looked at him expectantly. It was no pep rally but at least they were listening.

He continued, "Yes, that's right: you have the power, but before you rule the world there is one little favor you can do for us. It's not a big deal really-just help us get home. Then the wand is all yours and everyone goes away happy, okay?"

The buzzing sound returned as the goblins discussed this. Scott was puzzled by their lack of enthusiasm until Vex took the brothers aside and explained that the wand had been gone for so long; neither the goblins nor the knights knew how to use it. Although there was a prophecy about Ex Libris that had been passed from generation to generation, its meaning had been lost. The goblins found the prophecy to be more frightening than enlightening.

Vex then asked the obvious question. "Scott, if you used the wand to travel here, why don't you simply send yourselves back the same way?"

Scott looked embarrassed. Josh answered for him. "The truth is he doesn't know how we got here and he sure doesn't know how to get us home. Maybe we should hear this prophecy..."

Vex closed his eyes as if reaching into his memory for the exact words. Then in a singsong voice he began:

> *When fire streaks across the skies,*
> *And strangers are before your eyes,*
> *Beware Ex Libris will arise*
> *And bring about the end of days*
> *For all who live the warring way,*
> *But cunning, valor, strength and size*
> *United-will regain the prize.*
> *T'is life, not death, gives dragons breath,*
> *That is where the answer lies.*

"What the heck does that mean?" Scott wondered aloud.

Josh snapped his fingers, a trick he had just recently learned. "Scott, don't you get it? We are the ones who brought Ex Libris here so *we* must be the strangers in the prophecy!"

"You could be right Master Joshua. I only hope this is not the 'end of days'," Vex said sadly.

Scott stared at the ground, deep in thought. He finally looked up. "The only part that makes sense to me is that 'those who live the warring way' means the knights and the goblins need to stop fighting-or else. I don't understand the rest but I think I can figure out what 'Ex Libris' means. Whenever I do my crossword puzzles, 'ex' always means 'out of'-like the word 'exit'. 'Libris' means um..,'free'...no no, what am I saying, that's 'libre'. Is it 'scale'? No that's 'Libra' like the zodiac sign...wait, I've got it! 'Libris' is like 'library' so 'libris' means 'books'. 'Ex Libris' means 'out of books'."

Vex and Josh looked at him in amazement. "That was good dude," Josh complimented his brother.

"Of course!" Vex exclaimed. "The ancient Books of the Realm! Only one still exists, the Book of Lore but it's..."

"Is it lost?" asked Josh.

"No..." Vex hesitated, "It's hidden deep underground."

"Deeper than this?" Scott asked incredulously.

"Far deeper but that is not the problem. It is heavily guarded by a-"

"Not a dragon!" Josh interrupted.

Vex looked apologetic as he nodded. Josh threw his hands in the air.

"I knew it! I just knew it, *why* did it have to be a dragon?"

CHAPTER 7

Scott turned pale and broke into a sweat. "No way! I can't fight a dragon, not a real one anyway."

Josh patted his brother reassuringly on the shoulder.

"Don't worry Scott. That dragon won't stand a chance against the two of us."

"My dear friends," Vex said with a smile, "you don't have to *defeat* Talonfire! You simply need to snatch the book and bring it back here."

"Oh is that all we have to do?" Scott asked. "Sneak past a vicious dragon, steal his favorite book and then come back? Doesn't sound like a problem to me; does it sound like a problem to you Josh?"

Josh winced. "*Why* would we want to do that Vex?"

"Because you want to go home. Only with the Book of Lore can you learn the secrets Ex Libris holds. My hope is that Ex Libris can restore peace to our world and help us find the balance we lost."

Vex then proceeded to lay out a plan which seemed

doomed to fail. First, he would take them to the knights' castle. Once there, Scott and Josh had to convince the knights to show them the secret passageway into the dragon's lair. Vex warned them that the knights would refuse to help if they suspected the goblins were involved.

"They may refuse to help anyway," Vex added. "The knights are difficult and arrogant."

Once they had gained entrance to Talonfire's lair, Vex continued, Ex Libris would lead them to the Book of Lore. He was confident the wand would protect them, or at least protect Joshua, and for that reason recommended that Scott stick close to his brother.

"If we do manage to escape the dragon, with or without the book, how will we get back here?" Scott asked doubtfully.

"I haven't quite figured that out yet."

"And where are you during all of this?" Josh asked.

"It is best that I remain behind for my presence would only endanger your lives. You see, the knights have sworn vengeance against the goblins for the disappearance of Sir Gilcrest

"They believe we killed him."

Scott and Josh exchanged a look of uncertainty.

"Is it true?" Josh asked.

"Of course not! We are a peaceful people. Sir Gilcrest was our ruler as well; we would never have harmed him. With Ex Libris guiding him, he was a kind and benevolent leader for many years-until the day he began acting strangely. First he neglected his duties, then he disbanded the Council of Advisors and suddenly he was gone, never to be seen again. No one knows what happened to him."

"And Ex Libris?" asked Scott.

"Ex Libris went with him-or so we thought."

At that moment, two young goblins approached them. They bowed respectfully to Vex before the shorter one pleaded,

"Master Vxngrtl, please pardon our intrusion but we were sent to ask you, what is to be done? The goblins of the Cavern are frightened and need your guidance."

"Go back, my young friends, and tell the others... we have a plan."

CHAPTER 8

"I can't believe we're going along with this crazy scheme," Scott complained as they followed Vex back through the winding corridors. The orange bat-like creatures hanging along the walls hadn't moved since Scott last saw them.

"And you have a better plan?" Josh asked hopefully as he struggled with his backpack.

"I wish." Scott shifted his own backpack from one shoulder to the other.

"Vex, what is in these backpacks?" he groaned. "They weigh a ton. You said they were provisions but they better not be blue diamonds because I'm telling you now, I won't eat them!"

Josh piped in, "Would you eat them in a box? Would you eat them with a fox?"

Scott laughed despite himself.

"Don't worry about the weight Scott," Vex replied. "Once you're above ground, you'll be as light as air, just like before. As for the provisions, I wouldn't dream of packing blue diamonds for you to eat."

"Thank you."

"I packed *vegetables* instead." He chuckled. "I just thought a little humor would help the situation."

"Very funny. So, how are we getting out of this cavern? Or is that a secret too?"

"It's real high-tech Scott, it's called a ladder," Josh answered. "That's how I got down here, how did you get here?"

Vex glanced at Scott, his bushy eyebrows raised questioningly.

"I'd rather not talk about it," Scott replied, remembering how he tumbled down the hole screaming all the way.

It was a long tough climb out of the cavern but they finally reached the surface. Scott breathed a sigh of relief as the weightless feeling returned and the backpack stopped pressing on his shoulders. He found it comforting to see the bizarre yet familiar landscape; for some strange reason it made him feel closer to home.

"And now my intrepid explorers it is time to summon the vlats."

With this, Vex inserted two of his six blue fingers into his blue mouth and took a deep breath. Scott braced himself for a piercing whistle while Josh covered his ears. To their surprise there was no sound at all.

"I didn't hear anything, did you?" Josh asked his brother.

"The sound wasn't intended for your ears," Vex explained.

They could hear a faint whirring noise as if thousands of tiny wings were flapping. From deep inside the cavern a swarming orange cloud of vlats left their perch on the walls, flying higher and higher until they cleared the mouth of the cavern. The three travelers were soon surrounded by the delicate creatures.

"Let's go," Vex said seemingly unaware that his body was totally enveloped in shimmering vlats.

"Why are they bothering us? What do they want?" Scott asked shaking his arms and legs in an effort to escape the persistent vlats. Josh, on the other hand, was giggling at how much it tickled when they landed on him.

Vex shook his head in amusement. "What they want is to take us to our destination. There's no need to panic, they are quite harmless. In fact, it is because of the vlats that we are able to travel great distances. Now if you will just relax, they will carry you and your gear into the sky where you can experience the joys of flying. Ah, what a glorious thing! I envy you the thrill of flying for the first time, it is more exhilarating than you can ever imagine. Viewing the world from on high, soaring over the treetops, you will feel your cares drift away like a gentle rain falling to the ground."

"I'm ready!" Josh quickly replied.

"Sorry but you can count me out," Scott said, still trying to shoo the vlats away. "Flying sounds okay-it's crashing to the ground that worries me.

"Vex calmly explained that low gravity made flying perfectly safe but Scott just shook his head no. Vex then explained, a little less calmly, that the goblins had been flying this way for as long as anyone could remember. Scott stubbornly shook his head no again. Vex was becoming quite vexed indeed that he couldn't convince Scott to fly. It was only after Vex swore that NO-body had EVER crashed to the ground that Scott slowly nodded his head yes. Relieved, Vex asked the boys to prepare by standing still and holding their arms out at their sides. The vlats, like fluttering butterflies, began to land on them by the hundreds until all three of them were completely covered. Their clothes seemed to disappear, replaced by living orange suits that rippled like ocean waves as they moved.

Scott watched helplessly as his feet left the ground behind. Before he knew it, they were a flock of birds flying in V formation with Vex in front. The vlats flew together in rhythm, perfectly synchronized, with a swaying motion Scott found soothing. He felt like a baby being rocked to sleep. The fear he had been carrying around with him quietly slipped away. He seemed to be wrapped in a blanket of contentment and well-being. Vex looked back at him and smiled knowingly. Josh, who had never been afraid to fly, could barely contain his excitement and kept calling over to them with each new thing he saw. As Josh pointed, Vex would describe the landmark. To the far right were the crimson Mountains of Mimbar, to the left the turbulent Ocean of Norestia. The sparkling green lakes were the Lakes of Vantango and surrounding the lakes was the Living Forest.

There were no clouds here, fluffy or otherwise, and Scott regretted that he couldn't fly through one. He felt no wind or breeze but the air was cool and fresh and he couldn't get enough of it. Scott breathed so deeply he made himself light-headed and had to stop. Studying the terrain below, he could see that the bright blue grass was everywhere except where the yellow road curved through it. When he had walked there with Vex, Scott was convinced the road led nowhere, now he could see for himself it was true. He decided to keep this information to himself-sometimes there's just no satisfaction in being right. The strange pattern of the road intrigued him. Although he wasn't sure at first, he started to see that the loops in the road formed symbols. He recognized the letter "c" with a circle around it and then numbers, a two and three zeroes. It suddenly struck him that the road spelled "copyright" and the year 2000. That was the year "The Fight for Magicallus" came on the market! He wouldn't tell Vex about this discovery either, it would only upset him. Just then, Josh started yelling and pointing at the ground below.

"Look out! That Knight is about to attack us!"

CHAPTER 9

DIRECTLY BELOW THEM A SINGLE KNIGHT DRESSED IN full armor was riding hard on horseback, his face hidden behind his plumed helmet. In one hand he held a long sharp green lance, in the other a gleaming shield and the reins to control his steed. He was battle-ready yet seemed unaware of their presence.

"He's going to see us! Can't you make these vlats fly any faster?" Josh asked.

Vex appeared unconcerned.

"Why doesn't he look up? We're right above him," Scott was curious but not worried. Having lost his fear of flying, he now felt quite brave.

"Knights never look up; they only look forward as their helmets prohibit movement. I told you we have been flying this way for a long time. Encountering this chap out here has turned out to be a piece of luck for us, don't you see? Now, instead of traveling all the way to the castle and dealing with a dozen knights, you can stop here and converse with just one. I dare say your odds of prevailing have just greatly improved."

Josh looked doubtful. "I still don't like our chances."

"Both of you are brave and resourceful, I am confident you will succeed." Vex smiled at them encouragingly. "Just remember to keep the wand hidden at all times Master Joshua."

Then with a flick of his skinny blue fingers, he gestured to the vlats to follow the horse. Taking their cue from the goblin, the vlats pursued the rider at full speed, no longer delicate butterflies but fierce bats zooming in on their prey, wings whirring like propellers.

To say that Scott was no longer enjoying the ride didn't begin to describe his state of mind, as Josh was desperately trying to wriggle free of the crazed creatures. He would soon get his wish. Without any warning, the vlats retracted their silky grasp and let go. The boys began to spiral downward in slow motion like kites caught in a gust of wind, before landing gently on the weird rubbery grass. Unfortunately, they tumbled right into the Knight's path where the stallion's pounding hooves were about to crush Josh. Scott was quite sure Josh needed rescuing this time. He stood up quickly and, copying a wrestling move he had once seen, took a running start before head-butting his brother hard to push him out of the way.

Josh was thrown backwards quite a distance due to the low gravity, flipping over and over, like a human tumbleweed before finally coming to a stop. Remarkably, he was not the least bit grateful for Scott's assistance and used this opportunity to yell out some colorful new words. Scott would have been insulted had he not been so dazed from using his head as a battering ram. Got to remember not to do *that* again, he thought, rubbing his sore head.

When Scott looked up, he found a lance pointing at his chest and the silent menacing figure of the Knight standing over him.

After what seemed like forever, the Knight spoke.

"Friend or foe?" he demanded in a muffled voice.

"We're friends of the knights..." Scott said, holding his hands open to show he meant no harm.

The Knight snorted or at least that's what it sounded like from behind the helmet. He lowered the lance, no longer threatening.

"Friends you say? Ha! You are not *worthy* of that distinction. Just look at your attire! In the name of Sir Gilcrest, where is your honor? You have no armor or coat of arms-just like servants or peasants. Have you forgotten your weapons and horses as well? Why, you have no redeeming qualities that I can see...except you," he said grudgingly to Scott, "deserve some credit for saving the life of your puny friend. "

Josh jumped to his feet, facing off with the Knight," Who are you calling *puny*?"

The Knight threw his head back and laughed so loud his startled horse reared up on its hind legs and whinnied.

"Why, you are *both* puny-and quite foolish as well-but you are amusing, I will say that. What are your monikers pray tell?"

"Moniker?" Josh asked Scott, who just shrugged and shook his head.

"How do others address you?" The Knight asked, opening his visor to reveal a bushy black mustache perched above a wide mouth. He had large beaver-like front teeth and a pasty white complexion. There were no blue diamonds in that guy's diet, Scott thought. He found it quite strange to see the Knight's mouth moving without being able to see his eyes. It was like talking to someone wearing sunglasses, but worse. At least with sunglasses you would see a reflection of yourself, here there was nothing to look at but expressionless slits.

Scott pointed at his brother. "He's Josh and I'm Scott."

The Knight then introduced himself. "I am known as the

Heir to the Heladrian Empire, Keeper of the Royal Gate and Guardian to the Baron of Camembert."

Josh nodded his head excitedly. "Now I know you. You're Sir Edward the Fearless!"

"That is my common name, yes." He puffed his chest out and raised his chin. "I see that my excellent reputation has traveled far indeed. Not surprising given my many feats of bravery and acts of gallantry." His armor clanked as if agreeing with him.

"Yup, you're brave alright," Josh replied. "It's just too bad about that other guy."

"What are you talking about?" Scott hissed.

"You know," Josh answered in a loud voice, "the guy who's telling everyone he's braver than Sir Edward the Fearless."

The Knight jumped off his horse and pointed his lance at the sky. "Where is this knave, this scoundrel who besmirches my good name? I will teach him some manners!"

Scott wondered if Josh had lost his mind.

"Actually," Josh said, "we are here to give you a message from him. The message is that Lord Magic the Undefeated challenges you to a jousting match."

Scott gasped.

"Excellent!" Sir Edward shouted, his mustache quivering in anticipation. "A jousting match is just the thing to show who the superior knight is. I will vanquish that scurrilous scalawag. 'Lord Magic' indeed! When I am through with him, his name will be 'Lord Misery'. When shall we meet in battle? I am prepared to prove my valor this very moment."

Scott was pacing back and forth muttering under his breath. Josh paid no attention.

"He said he will meet you at the dragon Talonfire's lair. And since we are his...um... valets, we need to go too but we don't know the way. Can we go with you? That way the match won't be delayed," said Josh.

Sir Edward paused. "Why Talonfire's lair, I wonder? That is an odd place indeed for a jousting match. What if we disturb the dragon?" He stroked his moustache, lost in thought for a moment. "Very well, agreed. We shall leave at once."

CHAPTER 10

"Yes, this is *JUST* where I want to be," Scott whispered to Josh through gritted teeth, "riding on a wild horse with my crazy brother and an angry Knight who carries lethal weapons. What were you thinking?" As he spoke, his head jiggled to the rhythm of the horse's fast trot. He was hanging onto the saddle bags, which were really their backpacks, and trying not to fall off the horse.

"How else could we get him to take us there, you dweeb? Anyway, you didn't have a better plan."

"How would you know since you didn't bother to ask?" Scott retorted.

Josh was quiet for a while, hanging on tightly to Midnight's mane and enjoying the ride. He loved to go fast and this was much better than riding a skateboard or a bike.

"Look," he finally said keeping his voice low so the Knight wouldn't hear, "I'm sorry I didn't talk to you first but there was no time. You have to admit that my plan worked."

Scott shook his head. "Sir Edward is expecting a jousting match, remember? Are you going to fight him?"

"Nope."

"Then who is?"

"Nobody." Josh smiled mischievously. "Lord Magic is going to chicken out. Get it? That way Sir Edward will be happy that he's still the bravest Knight around and we can go find the book."

Scott had to admit it was ingenious, much better than anything he would have come up with but still he was annoyed. "Josh," he said, "tell me something. Why do you have to be so...so...*you?*

Josh shrugged. "Because I have to be myself, that's why. Besides," he said, making a silly face, "I *like* being me."

"Yeah I noticed," Scott said, laughing at his goofy brother.

They came to an abrupt stop and the boys almost tumbled off the horse.

"It's tea time," Sir Edward announced, helping them down. "Never go into battle without first taking tea I always say. I trust you brought some provisions? If not, you may share mine," he said, unpacking some sandwiches and a teapot from his leather saddlebag. He fed Midnight one of the sandwiches before digging into the bag for teacups and sugar cubes.

"Liverwurst sandwich?" he offered. "Or do you prefer herring?"

Scott tried hard to control his gagging reflex.

Josh politely declined. "Thanks but we brought our own."

They opened their backpacks not knowing what to expect and were overjoyed to see cheese sandwiches, potato chips and containers of juice. Other items in the packs were a long rope, some digging tools and several large blue diamonds. There was also a note: "I believe these items are within Scott's four food groups. Good luck in your quest, Vex. P.S. The blue diamonds are lights, *please don't eat them.*"

The spot Sir Edward had chosen for them to stop was

pleasant. A large rock served as their table and the smaller rocks around it were suitable chairs. The purple trees with orange leaves, which they learned were called maple berries, grew all around their rock table and provided a park-like atmosphere. When the Knight took off his helmet to eat, Scott was relieved to see that he looked fairly normal. His complexion was still pasty white but his intense dark eyes and long sharp nose caught your attention. Although his thick black hair hung to his shoulders, he couldn't be mistaken for a girl. Sir Edward invited them to take a seat and begin. The boys were very hungry and quickly ate everything they had. Sir Edward was a bit slower as he was drinking cup after cup of tea and quizzing them about Lord Magic.

"Has he performed any great feats? What do people say about him? Has anyone compared him to me?"

"You mean you haven't heard?" Scott hesitated, and then looked at Josh, who nodded. "Lord Magic slew...I mean slayed...um... he killed a fierce dragon in this awesome battle..."

Sir Edward leaped to his feet, furious. "He did what? It's outrageous! Killing the dragon is strictly forbidden by Rule 95; subsection D, of the Code of Errantry. He will pay for that! I'm afraid you two have chosen the wrong master to follow."

Scott turned to Josh and mouthed, "Oops."

"He had to do it," Josh said quietly, "the dragon was about to kill him."

The Knight immediately calmed down immediately. "Well, why didn't you say so in the first place? Killing a dragon in self-defense when one's own death is imminent is clearly permissible under Rule 58, subsection A. I am looking forward to meeting this fellow on the battlefield."

Then, as if nothing had happened, he began to pack up his things and wipe the crumbs off his mustache. Josh looked at Scott and shrugged.

"Sir Edward, when will we get to Talonfire's lair?" Scott asked a bit nervously.

He didn't answer but instead walked over to the widest mapleberry tree and pulled on one of its branches. Scott and Josh watched as a door appeared in the trunk. The Knight then pulled a branch on the opposite side of the tree and the door slid open to reveal a gloomy interior with stairs winding down into the darkness.

Sir Edward turned around to face them. "We are already there."

CHAPTER 11

"Where is he hiding?" Sir Edward bellowed, swinging his battleax. He was dressed in full armor again. "Where is that slanderous scoundrel? Lord Magic! Show yourself this instant!"

Josh whispered to Scott, "I feel...sick...I have this weird feeling in my stomach."

"I can understand why, with this big mess you've gotten us into," Scott whispered back, turning toward his brother. "Hey, you really don't look good, you know? Your face is kind of green and-"

Scott never had the chance to finish. As he watched, a thick green cloud of fog suddenly formed around Josh, lifting him off the ground and carrying him straight through the open door of the tree. Josh had been swept right into the dragon's lair! It happened so fast neither Scott nor Sir Edward had time to act and they gaped at the spot where Josh had been standing.

"What sorcery is this?" Sir Edward asked removing his visor for a better look.

Scott grabbed the knight's arm, his eyes wide with fright.

"You've got to help my brother; I can't save him by myself! *Please* come!"

"Your brother? Then he's your problem, not mine. Tell me why he entered Talonfire's lair, is he a sorcerer?"

"I can't explain it," Scott moaned. "You saw for yourself that he was dragged in there. It wasn't *his* idea." Scott was getting angry. "What's the deal with you anyway? Aren't knights supposed to rescue people? Maybe you're just afraid of the dragon..."

"How dare you!" the knight roared. "Sir Edward the Fearless fears nothing! I live to fight dragons, do you hear me? Now listen carefully, if I agree to rescue your brother, you must do exactly as I say, understood?" Scott nodded. "If you don't," he said with a dark look, "you will surely perish."

Scott shuddered.

Sir Edward turned his back on Scott and spoke to his horse. "Wait here my loyal steed. If anyone approaches, give me a signal. And I will hear you."

To Scott's surprise, Midnight nodded.

Hoisting his backpack on his shoulders, Scott followed Sir Edward through the secret door where icy cold air struck his face like a slap. He had never been so nervous before; his stomach was doing back flips and his heart was about to burst out of his chest. Too afraid to look around, Scott was only vaguely aware of the rocky walls around him. He was, however, acutely aware of the awful stench. It smelled just like the time his mom had burned dinner-fishy, burnt and smoky-all at the same time. He tried not to gag as he climbed down the narrow steps carved into the rock. The stairs seemed to go on forever. Scott had only covered about twenty steps when he heard a commotion back at the mouth of the cave. Midnight was braying like a donkey. Sir Edward had turned around and was racing back up the stairs almost knocking Scott over as he ran past. Scott quickly regained his balance and scrambled up after him. They both spotted the intruder at the same instant and chaos ensued.

Sir Edward shouted, "Vengeance is mine!" and lunged for the intruder.

Scott yelled out "No!" as he tackled Sir Edward and pinned him, face down, on the ground. The knight groaned loudly but did not try to get up.

The intruder spoke, "Thank you for your timely assistance. You really are quite brave you know."

Scott sighed as he sat on top of the knight, thinking that his nerves couldn't take much more of this. He asked the foremost question on his mind, "What are you doing here, Vex? I thought you said we were on our own."

Vex told Scott he had been following them all along. Although he had planned to stay out of sight, when he saw what happened to Josh he rushed right over.

"Strange and powerful forces are at work here Scott, but you may put your mind at ease your brother is safe. He is wrapped in a protective bubble called an aura which nothing can penetrate."

Scott was quite relieved to hear that Josh was not in immediate danger but couldn't answer Vex. He was too busy holding onto Sir Edward who had started struggling again. The knight lifted his head and spat out grass.

"Unhand me, you wretch!" he barked. Scott tightened his grip in response.

Reluctantly, Sir Edward muttered, "You have my word of honor that I won't harm either of you."

At this, Scott released him but stood ready to pounce again if necessary. The knight just sat up and shook his head, disgusted.

"Do you know this murderous traitor?" he asked Scott.

Scott nodded. Sir Edward's expression changed to one of disbelief.

"Surely this...this...*creature* isn't Lord Magic?"

Vex looked puzzled while Scott burst out laughing. Having a good laugh seemed to relieve some of Scott's tension. Although he still felt like a rubber band that had been stretched too far, he wasn't as close to snapping now.

"No," Scott assured him, "this isn't Lord Magic." He paused then said, "The truth is my brother Josh is Lord Magic."

It was Sir Edward's turn to laugh uproariously. "Your... brother?" he gasped, "That is impossible."

"It is true," Vex said. "He *did* slay the dragon Chimera..." Vex abruptly stopped talking and turned his head to listen.

Something was happening around them. There was an eerie silence. The yellow sky darkened to a bruised purple color and a powerful wind began to blow. Midnight whinnied with alarm. The silence was suddenly shattered when thunder erupted above them and fiery lightning ripped through the sky in dozens of places at once. Sir Edward tightly gripped Midnight's reins and the three of them held onto the trees to keep from being blown about like dried leaves. Above the din, Vex yelled out "The prophecy! It has come to pass!"

Scott yelled in response, "We must go back inside the dragon's lair."

Sir Edward followed them, pulling Midnight behind him. They dragged themselves from tree to tree fighting against the howling wind which blew them backwards. Finally, they reached the doorway and flung themselves through it. All was calm here. Scott couldn't believe he had willingly returned to this terrifying place.

The knight and goblin stood together uneasily in the entrance to the lair and Scott could feel the tension between them. He knew that even their present danger would not guarantee a peaceful coexistence-but he didn't have time to worry about it. He needed to focus on finding his brother.

"Don't you understand?" Vex cried out as he paced back and forth, "this is precisely what was foretold. Listen carefully to the words of the prophecy:

> *When fire streaks across the skies,*
> *And strangers are before your eyes,*
> *Beware Ex Libris will arise*
> *And bring about the end of days*
> *For all who live the warring way,*
> *But cunning, valor, strength and size*
> *United-will regain the prize.*
> *T'is life, not death, gives dragons breath*
> *That is where the answer lies."*

"That prophecy is balderdash!" Sir Edward declared. "It is meaningless drivel that only a foolish goblin would believe."

Vex was so angry that his bulging green eyes looked like they would pop right out of his head. Before he could respond, Scott stepped between them-only to have Midnight kick him in the shin.

"Ouch!" Scott complained, rubbing his leg. "Look Sir Edward, I know there's bad blood between you two but lay off the insults. Vex is onto something with this prophecy and I'll tell you why. First, correct me if I'm wrong but that sure looks like 'fire streaking across the skies', do you agree?" He pointed to the fearsome lightning still ripping through the sky.

"Yes but..." the knight started to say.

"Hold on, I'm not through. Second, have you ever seen me or my brother before today?"

"No."

"Are we strangers?"

"Yes but..."

"Then we *could* be the 'strangers before your eyes', right? Third-"

"Scott, no! You cannot tell him!" Vex pleaded.

"I'm sorry Vex but I need his help. Third, Ex Libris has most definitely 'arisen'. I brought it with me to Magicallus, well actually it brought me, and Josh has it now."

'Sir Edward was visibly shaken by this news. He staggered backwards against the damp mossy wall of the cavern and slid down until he was crouching on the floor. For once, he was speechless.

"Fourth," Scott began, waiting until he had Sir Edward's attention, "fourth, this *could* be the 'end of days'-but maybe not. It seems to me that we need to 'regain the prize' which I think is Ex Libris. To do that, we will need cunning, valor, strength and size. Between the three of us, we have all of those qualities. So, I need to know, are you in or are you out?"

Sir Edward nodded in silent agreement. Scott was pleased but clearly Vex was not. Leaving Midnight to guard the entrance once again, they began their descent into the lair. The knight walked in front and Vex brought up the rear. Scott thought it best that he walk between these two enemies. He had forgotten just how frigid the air was in the dragon's lair and he shivered. As they moved farther in, the terrible stench intensified. Visibility decreased to the point that they had to stop and retrieve Scott's blue diamonds from his backpack so they could see at all. A radiant blue light emanated from the diamonds which comforted the weary travelers. As they walked, they talked in low voices. Sir Edward explained that most dragons were unpredictable and angered easily. Usually, seeing a knight was enough to infuriate a dragon but Talonfire was different. No knight had ever battled with him and few had ever seen him, though many had tried.

After climbing down hundreds of steps, they finally reached the lair. It smelled horribly burnt and smoky and the floor was so slimy that they kept slipping. They could see debris all over the floor but couldn't make it out. After moving the light around, Scott realized the ground was covered with bones! He began shaking uncontrollably and started backing up in the direction of the stairs. He backed right into a wall where there hadn't been one before. Scott suddenly found himself ensnared, a dragon's tail wrapped tightly around his body.

He screamed out, "Vex! Help me!"

CHAPTER 12

Scott felt the dragon's fiery breath singe his hair before he saw it scorch the floor next to him. He stopped screaming and studied his captor. The dragon had a terrible beauty that Scott found fascinating, he couldn't bear to look yet he couldn't stop looking either. The beast was about ten feet tall and probably equally as long. Its skin was reddish-gold and scaly and so brilliant that it seemed to generate its own light. The dragon's eyes were quite frightening-like stars that had collapsed into black holes, they seemed to absorb everything yet reveal nothing. Its talons, all twenty of them, were deadly sabers and Scott realized that the dragon had spared his life by grabbing him with its tail. Although Vex was standing close by, he seemed paralyzed with fear. It was Sir Edward who sprang into action. Drawing his sword, he leaped forward and spoke to the dragon the way knights are taught to do.

"Talonfire, Awesome Beast, I pray you release your victim. He is not worthy of battle with you who are one of the Great Ones. It is I you must choose to battle, Sir Edward the Fearless,

Heir to the Heladrian Empire, Keeper of the Royal Gate and Guardian to the Baron of Camembert."

There was a long silence and Scott tried not to breathe too loudly or draw attention to himself in any way. Nonetheless, he felt the dragon's tail tighten around him. Sir Edward stood ready, his visor down, his sword held high. When Talonfire finally spoke, the sound of his raspy voice sent a deep rumbling throughout the cavern. Scott thought he had heard this same voice before in a scary movie-maybe it was "The Mummy".

"YOU ARE NOT THE ONE I SEEK."

Sir Edward lifted his visor and whispered to Vex, "Prepare to run on my mark."

But Vex showed no sign of having heard. The knight turned back to the dragon.

"With all due respect, Oh Great One, you are not following the Rules of Errantry at all. You simply cannot turn down a proper challenge. It just isn't done. The whole system could unravel if word of this leaked out."

His taunts were making the dragon furious and Scott wondered if Sir Edward was totally out of his mind. What was he thinking? Scott was even more scared now that he realized his life was in the hands of a lunatic. Talonfire erupted like a volcano. He roared until the walls shook, black smoke billowed from his nostrils and huge flames burst from his mouth. When the smoke cleared, Vex was sprawled on the ground, unmoving. Scott cried out. Sir Edward was on Talonfire's back, his sword at the dragon's throat pointing at the only spot unprotected by scales.

"Pity about the goblin," Sir Edward said without taking his eyes off the dragon. "Now release the boy or I will slay you."

Talonfire tried to shake him off but couldn't. Scott's respect for Sir Edward was increasing by the minute-he wasn't crazy after all. No wonder he was Josh's favorite knight. As soon as

Scott felt the dragon's grip begin to loosen, he wiggled free and ran over to Vex's side, crouching down beside his friend.

The knight pressed the sword deeper. "Where is the Book of Lore, Ancient One?"

Talonfire blinked, his eyes unfathomable. "GIVE ME THE ONE I SEEK. I WILL GIVE YOU THE BOOK."

"Who is it you seek?"

"THE ONE WHO KILLED MY MATE, THE ONE WHO KILLED CHIMERA!"

Scott shuddered; things had just gone from bad to worse. He feared for his brother. But where was Josh now? Sir Edward tirelessly held onto the dragon's throat and looked like he could keep it up indefinitely. Speaking to Talonfire in a slow, measured voice, the knight asked, "Why shouldn't I kill you first and then find the Book myself?"

"IT CANNOT BE FOUND."

To Scott's relief, Vex stirred at that moment and sat up. The goblin shakily rose to his feet and nodded at Sir Edward. He then placed two fingers in his mouth as if he would whistle but there was no sound. Scott hadn't expected one. Almost instantaneously, the flapping of hundreds of wings could be heard as an orange swarm of vlats dove into view. Vex gave them a signal and they dispersed to all parts of the dank cavern.

Scott was sure the vlats could find the Book of Lore, even in the dark. Like actors in a play before the curtain goes down, they stood as if posed: the knight threatening the dragon, the goblin looking off into the darkness and the boy watching and waiting.

When the vlats converged again, they flew together in a synchronized rhythm Scott recognized immediately. They were carrying something that was hidden from view. Landing next to Vex, the vlats gently released their prize: a glowing green bubble with Josh sleeping inside.

"Way to go Vex!" Scott shouted, doing a little victory dance. He vowed that if they ever got out of this mess, he would be nice to Josh no matter what.

"Scott, check your pocket," Vex said, sounding exhausted.

With a puzzled look, Scott complied. As he reached behind him, Ex Libris leaped out of his back pocket, where it had suddenly appeared, and into his left hand, making it tingle. At the sight of the wand, Talonfire bellowed as if he were in pain. With Sir Edward still on his back, the dragon charged toward Scott, fire pouring from his mouth.

CHAPTER 13

"Nooooo!" Scott was screaming. He crouched down, using his hands to shield his face from the dragon's flames. His left hand clutched the wand so tightly his nails were digging into his palm. At the same time, Sir Edward was on Talonfire's back, jabbing wildly with his sword at the dragon's neck but never coming close to the beast's vulnerable underside; he was barely able to hang on to the writhing creature.

Scott shook his head over and over before crying out, "I just want to go home!"

Suddenly all went quiet and dark. Scott wondered if he was dead, killed by the dragon. If he was dead, at least it didn't hurt. He sat there for a minute wondering where he could be when suddenly something jumped on him and scared him terribly. The thing had sharp claws and sharp little teeth and it was nibbling gently on his arm. Scott felt it lick his face.

"Sunny!" he yelled out, hugging his dog and laughing. "How did you get here?"

Then he heard his mother calling to him, "Scott, please take the dog out before we eat dinner."

Scott fumbled for the light switch and flipped it on. Yes, this was definitely his room. He was home! Ex Libris had done this but Scott didn't understand how. Maybe he had been home the whole time and none of it had even happened. He studied the wand in his hand for clues but none appeared. Scott looked nervously over at the computer monitor on his desk and groaned. There on the screen was Talonfire bucking like a rodeo bronco with Sir Edward riding him like a cowboy. Despite the knight's valiant efforts to stop him, the dragon was still charging forward. But why? With Scott gone, who could the dragon be attacking? Scott gasped. It was Josh! With its deadly teeth, Talonfire had picked up the glowing green ball that held Scott's brother and hurled it against the wall. Vex was urgently trying to signal the vlats to help Josh but the dragon saw what he was doing and swatted him across the lair.

Scott's palms were sweating as he grabbed the controller and started working all the buttons. Nothing happened. Holding up the wand, he said "I just want Josh to go home!" Again nothing happened. Then he had an idea; he wasn't sure if it would help but it seemed worth a try. After searching for one particular button on the keyboard, Scott carefully pushed it. It worked! The pause button made everyone on the monitor freeze where they stood, even Josh in his aura, was poised in mid-air like an instant replay of a winning goal. With a deep sigh of relief, Scott sat back in his chair to think.

If he could go back the same way, he would grab his brother and come home. Simple enough, so long as the dragon stayed in "pause" position. He checked out the monitor, nobody had moved. Scott held Ex Libris high and said, "I just want to go to Talonfire's lair," and he was there.

Coughing from the awful smell and shivering from the freezing air, Scott marched over to his brother Josh-who could now be referred to as "bubble boy"-and jumped up to grab him.

THE FIGHT FOR MAGICALLUS

Unfortunately, Scott couldn't quite reach high enough to get a grip on the aura. After jumping a dozen times without success, he decided to try to pop the bubble. He jumped again, this time with the wand pointing up. As soon as Ex Libris touched the aura, green sparks came cascading down and the aura floated gently to the ground where it dissolved on contact. Scott shook Josh. "Wake up!" he insisted, but Josh kept on snoring. Only after Scott pinched him and pulled his hair did Josh roll over and stretch.

"Leave me alone, you dweeb. I don't want to go to school. I want to sleep!"

Josh opened his eyes just a little bit, then wider and wider. "Is this a nightmare? Why are we in this disgusting place?"

"Long story, no time. C'mon, we need to go." Scott said, tugging his brother's arm.

"But what about Vex, we can't leave him like that." Josh said gesturing toward the goblin curled up in a corner of the cavern, in "pause" position.

Scott looked agitated. "This is just a game, you know? We don't belong here. They managed fine before we came; they'll manage fine after we're gone."

Josh looked his brother in the eye. "Vex is our friend, we have to help him."

Scott stared back, then blinked and looked away. "Yeah, you're right. I guess even you can be right once in a while." He winked at his brother. "Let's try to unfreeze him and then we'll go." They went over to Vex and touched him with the wand. The goblin opened his eyes, jumped to his feet and, without a word, embraced them both. His touch gave them both a mild shock but they didn't care.

"Master Joshua, I am glad to see you're awake," he said smiling. "You are one of the privileged few who have slept the perfect sleep of the aura." He turned to Scott who looked embarrassed that he had hesitated to help-but Vex didn't notice "Scott, I believe I know what you must do. Hold the wand up with your left hand while your brother holds it with his right hand. Ex Libris needs both of you to restore the balance. This small gesture should be enough to break all spells."

When they did as Vex suggested, the brothers felt a warmth move from their fingers through their bodies-but nothing seemed to happen. Josh let go and when he turned around, he shouted for his brother. Although Sir Edward hadn't moved, he was no longer on Talonfire's back. The dragon had disappeared and Sir Edward was now riding on the back of a man. The man, who was also "paused" and unmoving, had straggly blond hair and tattered clothing. His expression was one of fury but, despite this, there was something regal about him, like he used to be somebody. Vex quietly directed them to unfreeze the others and they complied. Facing the stranger, Vex bowed to the ground.

Sir Edward tumbled off his perch, saw the stranger and dropped to one knee with his head lowered. "My Liege, how may I serve you?"

The angry man glared at all of them for a long minute and then his expression gradually softened, as if he remembered something long forgotten.

"Arise," he said, his voice deep and resonating "I am not worthy of your loyalty. I am not who you think I am."

Scott and Josh looked puzzled. Suddenly Josh understood.

"You're Sir Gilcrest, aren't you?" he asked.

"I was."

"And now?" Scott asked.

"I am Talonfire. When I was Gilcrest, I lusted for power until it consumed me. I studied the Book of Lore and used Ex Libris for my own purposes. I cast a spell to make myself all-powerful and I was transformed into a dragon. I forgot how to be a man and I sought a mate, another dragon named Chimera. When you killed her," he looked at Josh with great sadness, "I swore to avenge her death but I seek vengeance no more." Scott could see that Josh was greatly relieved by this announcement.

Vex spoke. "Will you lead us again? We are in great need of your wisdom."

"I cannot."

"Now I understand," Scott said. They all looked at him. He explained. "The prophecy means that the goblins and the knights must achieve peace on their own, even without Sir Gilcrest. Vex, Sir Edward," he nodded to them, "the two of you will reunite your people. You are both wise leaders and if you rule together, your people will follow."

Vex bowed his head respectfully to Sir Edward. Sir Edward bowed back.Sir Gilcrest turned to Scott, "I will bring you the Book of Lore."

"I don't think we need it anymore," Scott said. "I know how to get back but there's still something we need to do before we go." He gestured to Josh to hold the wand with him and then he recited the prophecy:

> When fire streaks across the skies,
> And strangers are before your eyes,
> Beware Ex Libris will arise
> And bring about the end of days
> For all who live the warring way,
> But cunning, valor, strength and size
> United-will regain the prize.
> T'is life, not death, gives dragons breath
> That is where the answer lies.

As Scott uttered the last word, a cloud of green smoke

appeared. When it cleared, they saw a dragon materialize out of nowhere.

"Chimera! My soul mate!" Sir Gilcrest cried out. He looked beseechingly at Scott and Josh and they touched him with the wand, transforming him back into Talonfire.

As they watched the dragons fly away together, Vex and Sir Edward thanked the boys for all they had done, promising that a new era had arrived for the goblins and the knights. They all embraced. As Scott and Josh prepared to go, Vex whispered to them "Please take care of *The Fight for Magicallus* game for us. And Scott..."

"Yes Vex?"

"Don't forget to eat your vegetables."

"Yeah, right," Scott said with a grin. "That'll happen. We need to get going."

The brothers held onto the wand together and Scott said, "We just want to go home," and they were home, back in Scott's room.

Their Mom walked in the door, drying her wet hands on a dish towel she was holding.

"Hey guys, what are you two doing? You've been so quiet, I decided to check on you."

The boys exchanged a look and Josh said, "We were trying to find a book to read."

She beamed at them. "You don't know how happy that makes me. C'mon, let's eat dinner, Dad just got home."

She glanced at Scott's hand. "What's with the magic wand, Scott? You planning to make your brother disappear or something?"

Scott winked at Josh and said, "I'm thinking about it."

THE END

Dear reader,

We hope you enjoyed reading *The Fight For Magicallus*. Please take a moment to leave a review, even if it's a short one. Your opinion is important to us.

Discover more books by Barbara Venkataraman at https://www.nextchapter.pub/authors/barbara-venkataraman

Want to know when one of our books is free or discounted? Join the newsletter at http://eepurl.com/bqqB3H

Best regards,
Barbara Venkataraman and the Next Chapter Team

Award-winning author Barbara Venkataraman is an attorney in South Florida where she draws inspiration for her books from the daily headlines. She loves connecting with readers through her books and finds a particular kind of joy in a well-turned phrase. In addition to writing fiction, she co-authored *Accidental Activist: Justice for the Groveland Four* with her son Josh Venkataraman about his successful four-year quest to obtain posthumous pardons for The Groveland Four.

The Fight For Magicallus
ISBN: 978-4-86752-784-9

Published by
Next Chapter
1-60-20 Minami-Otsuka
170-0005 Toshima-Ku, Tokyo
+818035793528

6th August 2021